CHESE BOOKS, INC.
Author: ...PART 5
... Chinese Books is a member of Complete Lunar, Inc.
... is not ... by the U.S. Patent and Trademark Office
... no part ... be ... by any ... stock ... copied
... M ... Printed in Mexico, ... in U.S.A.

Mother Goose
Rhymes

Hush-a-bye, baby, on the tree top!
When the wind blows the cradle will rock;
When the bough breaks the cradle will fall;
Down will come baby, bough, cradle and all.

This little pig went to market;
This little pig stayed at home;
This little pig had roast beef;
This little pig had none;
This little pig said, "Wee, wee!
I can't find my way home."

Little Bo-Peep has lost her sheep,
And can't tell where to find them;
Leave them alone, and they'll come home,
And bring their tails behind them.

There was a crooked man,
And he went a crooked mile,
He found a crooked sixpence
Beside a crooked stile;
He bought a crooked cat,
Which caught a crooked mouse,
And they all lived together
In a little crooked house.

There was an Owl lived in an oak,
Whiskey, Whaskey, Weedle;
And all the words he ever spoke
Were Fiddle, Faddle, Feedle.

Simple Simon met a pieman,
Going to the fair;
Says Simple Simon to the pieman,
"Let me taste your ware."
Says the pieman to Simple Simon,
"Show me first your penny,"
Says Simple Simon to the pieman,
"Indeed, I have not any."

Little Boy Blue,
Come, blow your horn!
The sheep's in the meadow,
The cow's in the corn.
Where's the little boy
That looks after the sheep?
Under the haystack, fast asleep!

Jack and Jill went up the hill,
To fetch a pail of water;
Jack fell down, and broke his crown,
And Jill came tumbling after.

Mary had a little lamb,
Its fleece was white as snow;
And everywhere that Mary went
The lamb was sure to go.
He followed her to school one day —
That was against the rule;
It made the children laugh and play
To see a lamb at school.

Pat-a-cake, pat-a-cake, baker's man;
So I will, master, as fast as I can:
Pat it, and prick it, and mark it with B,
Put it in the oven for Baby and me.

Old Mother Hubbard
Went to the cupboard,
To give her poor dog a bone;
But when she got there
The cupboard was bare,
And so the poor dog had none.

The Queen of Hearts,
She made some tarts,
All on a summer's day;
The Knave of Hearts,
He stole the tarts,
And took them clean away.